The illustrations for this book were done in acrylic, ink, and pencil on plywood.
The text was set in Gararond Medium, and the display type is Aram Caps.
Design by Saho Fujii and Neil Swaab

RED KNIT CAP GIRL

by

NAOKO STOOP

Megan Tingley Books
LITTLE, BROWN AND COMPANY
New York   Boston

In the forest, there is time to wonder about everything.
Red Knit Cap Girl wonders about flowers, butterflies, leaves, and clouds.

But most of all, Red Knit Cap Girl wonders about the Moon.
"Could I ever get close enough to the Moon to talk to her?"

"Maybe I could reach her this way."
She tries, but the branch isn't long enough.

"Or could I reach her that way?"
But the Moon isn't in the water.
It is just a reflection.

It seems the Moon is just too far away.
Red Knit Cap Girl sighs.

After a while, Hedgehog comes by.
"Owl knows everything," he says.
"Ask him how to reach the Moon."

"Where can we find him?" she asks.

"He is in the hollow of the oldest oak tree."

Red Knit Cap Girl holds on tight to
White Bunny.
"Mr. Owl? We have a question for you."
Owl does not answer.

Red Knit Cap Girl tries again.
"Please, Mr. Owl, can you tell us how we can get close enough
to talk to the Moon?"

Owl comes out slowly and says,
"The Moon is too far to reach, but if you want, she will
bend down to listen to you."

"But how will she know I'm waiting for her?"
asks Red Knit Cap Girl.

"You will find a way."

Owl smiles and flies off on his silent wings.
Red Knit Cap Girl thinks for a moment.
She knows what she needs to do.

"Everyone, I have an idea. We need to show the Moon we are looking for her,"
says Red Knit Cap Girl.
"Tonight, when she comes out, let's have a celebration!"
Her friends are all delighted.

They talk about what the Moon would like.

"The Moon might like decorations," says Hedgehog.

"I can hang them because I am tall," says Bear.

"I can help because I am nimble," says Squirrel.

Red Knit Cap Girl makes lanterns out of paper,
and everyone helps to hang them.

In the evening, they light the lanterns
and sit on a branch to wait for the Moon.

They sing for the Moon as they wait for her.
They wait and wait for the Moon to appear.

But she is nowhere to be seen.

"That's strange," says Hedgehog.
"The Moon always comes out at night."

"She might be too shy," says Squirrel.

"She might have gone somewhere else," says Bear.

"We should wait a little longer,"
says Red Knit Cap Girl.

But there is just silence.

Suddenly, they hear Owl from high up on a branch.
"The Moon is there."

"Mr. Owl, if the Moon is there, why can't we see her?"

Just then, a gust of wind blows out
one of the paper lanterns, and
a star appears in the dark sky.
"Ah!" Red Knit Cap Girl exclaims.
"I know what to do!"

She turns to her friends.
"Everyone, please be quiet
and take a deep breath.
Now, are we ready?"

The moment the lights are blown out,
all the forest grows dark and quiet.
And . . .

...the Moon comes out at last.
"There you are!" says Red Knit Cap Girl.

The Moon smiles and says,
"You have made it dark enough to
see me and quiet enough to hear me,
Red Knit Cap Girl."

Red Knit Cap Girl whispers to the Moon.

The Moon smiles quietly.

Together, they listen to the sounds of the forest.

Now Red Knit Cap Girl knows the Moon will always be there for her.